PONY CAMP

diaries

Jessica and Jewel

For all you fabulous Pony Camp fans everywhere, with love xx

tiger tales

5 River Road, Suite 128, Wilton, CT 06897
Published in the United States 2020
Originally published in Great Britain in 2007
by the Little Tiger Group
Text copyright © 2007, 2020 Kelly McKain
Illustrations copyright © 2007, 2020 Mandy Stanley
ISBN-13: 978-1-68010-452-3
ISBN-10: 1-68010-452-7
Printed in China
STP/1800/0311/1119
10 9 8 7 6 5 4 3 2

For more insight and activities, visit us at www.tigertalesbooks.com

PONY CAMP
diaries

Jessica and Jewel

by Kelly McKain

Illustrated by Mandy Stanley

tiger tales

Other titles in the series:

THIS DIARY BELONGS TO

Contents

Dear Riders,

A warm welcome to Sunnyside Stables!

Sunnyside is our home, and for the next week it will be yours, too! We're a big family—my husband, Jason, and I have two children, Olivia and Tyler, plus two dogs ... and all the ponies, of course!

We have friendly yard staff and a very talented instructor, Sally, to help you get the most out of your week. If you have any worries or questions about anything at all, just ask. We're here to help, and we want your vacation to be as enjoyable as possible—so don't be shy!

As you know, you will have a pony to take care of as your own for the week. Your pony can't wait to meet you and start having fun! During your stay, you'll be caring for your pony, improving your riding, enjoying long rides in the country, learning new skills, and making new friends.

And this week's special activity is a cowboy-style trail ride and campout under the stars—yee-haw! Add swimming, games, movies, barbecues, and a gymkhana, and you're in for a fun-filled vacation to remember!

This special Pony Camp Diary is for you to fill with your vacation memories. We hope you'll write all about your adventures here at Sunnyside Stables—because we know you're going to have a lot of them!

Wishing you a wonderful time with us!

Jess xx

Monday—a little past 9 a.m.
I've just arrived here at Pony Camp!

My little sister Tegan and I are the first ones
here because Mom had an early meeting and
she needed to drop us off beforehand. Jess
(the nice lady who runs Pony Camp) is still
busy figuring out all the sleeping arrangements
upstairs, so we're sitting at the kitchen table
at the moment. She gave us some juice and
drawing stuff to keep us busy, and
these cool Pony Camp Diaries, one
each, which is what I'm writing in
right now. Tegan is drawing a fairy
with pink wings, but also skinny
jeans like mine and furry boots.

I'm so excited about Pony
Camp! I can't wait to find out which
pony I'm getting, and spending a
whole week riding will be fantastic!

I usually go to the stables on Saturday mornings (Tegan comes, too), and I'm not great or anything, but I know the basics. I can walk, trot, and canter and do some of the trickier transitions like halt to trot (well, sometimes, if I'm on Molly!). I've even tried some jumping on Gingersnap, including a few combinations. My instructor Jane tries to switch us each week so we get a lot of experience on different ponies. That's great, but it'll be so exciting to have the same pony all this week, as if he (or she!) is actually mine!

Oh, it's going to be so *COOL!* —I'll have my own pony, and be sharing a room with girls my own age! At home I have to share with Tegan, which means I'm always tripping over her dolls, and she's always taking my glitter eyeshadow and wasting TONS! And it means NO noise after 7:30 p.m. when she goes to bed—so no video games or TV or music. I'm allowed my bedside lamp on to read, but I even have to turn the pages of my book quietly!

I'm super into boarding school books at the moment, and I'm extra excited because this week will be just like boarding school, but even better 'cos we'll have ponies. I've bought tons of stuff for a midnight snack and I've been saving up a few really juicy secrets to tell when we do our whispering in the middle of the night.

And I chose to come especially this week because there's going to be a trail ride and campout! I've always been into cowboys and western stuff, so going on a real trail ride is a dream come true! Getting to trek through miles and miles of open country, and camping out under the stars, and having hot dogs and beans, and singing around the fire will be so exciting!

Yee-haw!

Tegan isn't bothered about the trail ride, or even about ponies that much, but of course as soon as I showed Mom the brochure for Pony Camp,  my sister wanted to come, too. Mom and Dad were definitely agreeable to that, because if we both went, it meant they could have a break away on their own, so they're off to New York City tomorrow. I said, "What about *me* having a vacation by myself without Tegan?"

Mom laughed and replied, "Well, Dad and I haven't had a vacation by ourselves since before you were born, so I figure we get priority, don't you, Jess? Anyway, think about your sister. She'd much rather be with you and a lot of other girls than just us two."

Mom doesn't understand and, well, it is hard to explain. It's not like I *mind* T being here, but it's ... well, I kind of just want to be me, Jess, and do my own thing, without having to worry about taking care of her for a change. I mean, of course I like doing things with her, she's my little sister, but she's 7 and I'm 10 and a half, so it's not exactly as though we enjoy the same things. She always wants me to play these made-up games with her, like school or doctor, and sometimes they go on for hours. Mom and Dad run a mail order business together, and they're usually in their office (i.e., the spare room), and they're always saying "in a minute" and "I just need to finish this," so I'm left doing stuff with Tegan a lot of the time.

Oh, well—we're both here now and that's that, so there's no point complaining about it. Hopefully there'll be some younger girls she can make friends with.

I can't wait for everyone else to get here so Pony Camp can really get started! Then I'll have TONS to write about!

I'm quickly writing this while everyone's getting their stuff unpacked

Can you believe it? Tegan and I have been put in a room together because we're sisters. All my sleepover plans are completely ruined, and it's going to be just like it is at home (i.e., BORING!).

ARGH!

When everyone started arriving, Jess showed us all upstairs, and there were these three really awesome older girls and three younger, and I thought, oh, good, two rooms of four, so I can go in with the older ones. But then it turned out there are actually three rooms and that I'm sharing with Tegan.

I really wanted to ask if I could go in with the older girls instead, but I didn't want to seem like a complainer, and anyway there are no spare beds in there, so I tried to act like

I didn't mind. In addition to our bunk bed,
there's a single bed by the window. Jess said
it was her daughter Olivia's, and I cheered up
'cos I thought, *Well at least we'll be sharing
with someone else.* But then she said Olivia's
away this week staying with her aunt, so it
really is only going to be me and Tegan. All
my imaginings about midnight snacks and
whispering girly secrets went poof out of my
head and I just stood there feeling glum, until
Tegan brought me back to reality by making a
big deal about having the top bunk.

Unpacking my stuff on the bottom bunk did cheer me up a bit, though. I kept thinking, *Wow, I'm actually here at Pony Camp—and staying for a whole week!* I don't suppose sharing with T will be all that bad. Maybe when she goes to sleep, I'll be able to sneak into the older girls' room for midnight snacks so I don't completely miss out. I'm definitely not going to let it stop me from enjoying this week, anyway. After all, I can't wait to meet my pony, and there's the trail ride to look forward to, and all the lessons and helping out in the yard (and mucking out—ugh—hee-hee!).

Oh, we're being called downstairs now—time to go and meet the other girls, and find out which pony I'm getting!

Pony Camp is AWESOME!

I've really, REALLY cheered up now 'cos I've
had the most fantastic day!

I'm writing this in our free time after dinner.
We were supposed to go swimming next,
but the sky looks a bit grumbly-thundery. Jess
wants us to hold off for a while to wait and
see what the weather does, so I'm sitting
at one of the picnic
benches outside the
barn. Claudia, Bailey,
and Danni (the
three older girls I
mentioned before)
are here with me, writing in
their Pony Camp Diaries, too!

The younger girls are in the game room
doing something (I'm not quite sure what),

but Tegan's here with us. She didn't want to write in her diary 'cos she's not that fast at writing, and she's already done a pic of her pony, Twinkle, so she's making a giant daisy chain on the grass instead. Oh, there's so much to write—I'd better go back to where I left off.

We got down to the yard and Jess introduced us to Sally, the other instructor, and Lydia, the stable girl who'll be helping us with our ponies this week. Then Sally got us to say our names, our ages, and where we're from. Claudia is 12 and from Chicago, Danni's actually 13 and from Chicago, too. (How cool! She's a teenager!) Bailey is 10 and a half like me, and she flew all the way over here from Miami especially for Pony Camp this week (all on her own, how brave!) 'cos she wanted to go to a real riding school like she reads about in pony books.

Bailey   Claudia   Danni

When it was Tegan's turn, she gave me a
panicky look, so I introduced both of us. She's
not really shy or anything, but she does get
a little tongue-tied with new people. When
Danni said she liked my top, I felt great 'cos
she's about the coolest girl I've ever seen
(except on television). I love her swishy
sideways bangs and the leather bracelets she
wears all up her arm. And I love the way she
spells her name, too. I've been trying out a
few different ways of spelling Jess on my hand
(and even my full name, Jessica), but
it doesn't really work.

Jessi

Jessika

Jess-E-ka

23

The younger girls are Summer and Alicia, who are both just 8, and Lola, who's 7.

Tegan should have fit in perfectly with them 'cos she's 7, too, but she clung on to me the whole time, even when Sally showed us around the yard and gave us the safety talk. But luckily, Lydia brought Tegan's pony out (a beautiful yellow dun named Twinkle), and she fell completely in love with him and forgot I existed!

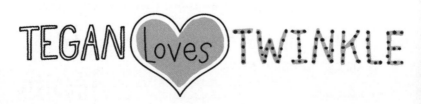

Then I met my totally gorgeous pony, Jewel.
Here's her profile:

 # Jess's Pony Profile

NAME: Jewel
AGE: Sally's not exactly sure,
but she thinks about 8.
HEIGHT: 13.2hh
BREED: Part-Welsh
COLOR/MARKINGS: Beautiful shiny chestnut with a
flowing mane and strong white blaze that arches
cutely over one of her eyes.

Sally says Jewel came from her friend
Bob's ranch as a loan for the final week of
last summer. It worked out so well that they
decided to have her back again this year. She's
only here for a week, and I'm the lucky girl
who gets to ride her! Sally also mentioned that
Jewel is trained as a western pony (although
she totally understands what I'm asking for
when I ride her the English way, too).

This is who everyone else got paired up with:

Claudia + Sparkle

Danni + Fisher

Summer + Sugar

Lola + Monsoon

Me + Jewel

Bailey + Flame

Alicia + Prince

Tegan + Twinkle

All the other girls fell in love with their
ponies right away, just like I did!

Jewel is my perfect pony—really
gentle and sweet with plenty of
spirit and stamina. I just know she's
a wild western girl at heart like me.
I'm sure we'll both love the trail ride!

We had a great time in the assessment
lesson 'cos she's so easy to ride. We did a
long warm-up with tons of trotting and circles
and changes of direction and no stopping
for a rest. Sally said we all have to build up
stamina for the trail ride, where we'll be
riding for several hours each day. The best
part was when we cantered around to the
back of the ride. (Well, me and the older
ones did—Tegan and the younger ones just
went around in trot again.) We had to make
sure we stopped in time so we didn't spook
the pony in front of us. Sally said this will

be extra important when we're out in the countryside cantering as a group. The lesson made me even more excited about the trail ride! Oh, I hope we can have lassoes and wear cowboy hats for it, but I don't think we'll be allowed!

Afterward, we took our ponies back to the barn, and Lydia helped us untack. Once we'd chugged at least two cups of water each in the kitchen, we hurried back to the yard to find out from Sally what group we'd be in. As I was hoping, I'm in group B with the older girls. That means I should be able to push myself a bit this week. My instructor at home wanted me to move up a group last month, but I couldn't because me and Tegan have to go together. (Mom says she can't drive there and back twice.)

We did some yard work before lunch. Bailey was helping me to sweep up, and we were

singing that new Sheana song while we were working. We tried out the harmonies and everything—and it sounded so cool!

Tegan finished scrubbing out the feed buckets, as Lydia had asked her to, and then she was just hanging around near me (kind of like she is now, in fact!). So I said, "Hey, why don't you go and run the wheelbarrow up the muck heap with Lola and Alicia?"

Tegan looked over and saw those two collapsing in a heap of giggles while trying to steer the big heavy wheelbarrow down the bumpy road, and her eyes lit up. "Can we?" she asked.

She looked so excited that I didn't have the heart to say, "I didn't mean me and you, I just meant you."

Bailey said it was no problem and that she'd finish up the sweeping, so I went with Tegan. It was fun, but I felt a little frustrated about having to leave Bailey right when we were getting the song perfect.

Our lesson this afternoon was really cool because we did jumping! Sally said it might help us later on in the week, but when we asked why, she got all mysterious and wouldn't say. She definitely has a surprise up her sleeve! She put up a couple of combinations—a single and three strides, then a double and two cross poles with only a bounce in between them. Jewel went over really smoothly, but I need to work on going with her rhythm and sensing when to bob up, instead of trying to count strides and getting in a pickle.

U Jessica and Jewel U

Sparkle did a couple of good jumps, but then this gate crashed in the wind and she got completely spooked, so she kept running out after that. Sally chose me and Jewel to give Claudia a lead over a practice jump and get Sparkle back on track. I was a bit nervous 'cos I've only recently started jumping myself and I didn't think I could lead anyone else, but my beautiful pony kept calm and made sure it all went smoothly.

Sparkle soon got her confidence back, and Claudia was really grateful and kept saying thanks to me, even after the lesson when we were untacking back in the yard. I said it was mostly Jewel being amazing, but Claudia insisted it was me, too. Maybe she's right and I'm a better rider than I realized!

On the way back to the farmhouse for dinner, Claudia linked arms with me. I felt really cool walking along beside her because she's so grown up and beautiful. I'm leaning this book a little away from her as I'm writing this—I want her to think I find it totally normal to have

older girls as friends, not something worth writing about! But then Tegan ran up and linked arms on the other side of me,  and when we got inside, she made me go to the bathroom with her and wait outside the door, even though it's only upstairs and not spooky at all. Oh, well, I'm sure she'll stop sticking to me so much when she settles in a little and gets more comfortable.

Hey! **YUCK!** It just started raining— gotta go, or this page will turn into mush!

Still Monday—in bed

Well, it really poured in the end, so it was lucky
we hadn't gone in the pool after all! Instead, we
hung out in the game room, and Jess put out
different things, like board games and the dance
mats, and there was table tennis, too. Alicia and
Summer got really into that and
kept playing for so long that their
wrists must have been almost
falling off. I played Tegan's favorite
game with her for a while. She
would have gone on all night, but I didn't want
to because I want to do new things at Pony
Camp, not the same old stuff.

Tegan insisted on putting all the
pieces back in exactly the right place, which
was taking forever, so I went on the dance
mats with Bailey and Danni for a while. Then
we started playing this wheelbarrow game

with Claudia where you hold each other's legs and walk on your hands. We all took turns at being the wheelbarrow and being the driver and got really giggly, especially because Bailey and Claudia kept going all crooked and almost ran into each other!

Me ↓

Danni

Claudia ↓

↑ Bailey

Then I got an idea for a game from watching Summer and Alicia earlier on. We made a pile out of the couch cushions and tried to go up it. Of course, we ended up in a heap on the floor in hysterics. I felt great that I'd made up the

game and they were having such a good time
playing it.

Tegan wanted to join in and be my
wheelbarrow, but then Bailey would have
been left out, which would have spoiled it. So
instead, I tried to get T interested in playing
with the younger girls by saying, "Oh, wow! I
can't believe Lola has the latest Starshine pony
and the showjumping school! I bet you'd love
to help her and Alicia set up a course!" But
she still wouldn't go.

Luckily, Jess soon sent her up to get in the
shower, so she wasn't hanging around on her
own for very long. Well, not that long, anyway.
And pretty soon after that I had to go up for
mine, too.

Oh, there's Jess. Time for lights out. Good
night!

Tuesday morning (early!)—
ugh, I'm so tired! ☹

I hardly got any sleep last night because Tegan insisted on squishing into my bed with me, even though she actually chose the top bunk—typical! She thrashed around all night, keeping me awake—probably dreaming of riding Twinkle. I had to move up to her bed to get any peace!

z ARGH! w

This isn't how I imagined Pony Camp nights at all! I wanted to be telling sleepover secrets and having midnight snacks with girls my own age, but instead I've ended up getting kicked all night because my little sister sneaked into my bed!

Well, never mind. I'll creep out and visit my friends tonight once Tegan's asleep! Oh, that's my alarm clock going off. I bet I'll be the first one up and dressed!

Tuesday—I'm writing this after lunch while Bailey and Danni are on dishwashing duty

We had a really fun lecture this morning on colors, breeds, markings, and points of the horse. (Well, points of the *pony*, because Lydia demonstrated on Prince!) After the demo, she set a little competition. We had to go around the yard visiting all the ponies and seeing how many different colors and markings we could find. It was a great excuse to make a big fuss of them all! I went with Claudia (and Tegan, of course—she was supposed to go with Summer but she wouldn't leave me, so the younger ones ended up in a three). We got a *ton*, including blue roan and yellow dun colors (i.e., Twinkle) and stockings as well as socks. Bailey and Danni still managed to find the most, though (they'd gone up to the field and counted in some of

♡ Pony Camp Diaries ♡

the horses, too—sneaky!). So they won and got a clap at the end and a chocolate bar each.

Our lesson was great, too—we did flat work this morning, with another long, tough warm-up, including a lot of turns, circles, and changes of rein to really get our ponies listening. Then we went on to balance exercises, which Sally says will help on the trail ride when we're going over rough ground. Thinking about that makes me feel so excited—I can't wait for tomorrow! We tried riding without stirrups, which was so easy on Jewel because she just glides around really smoothly—even while she was trotting, I didn't get a sore bum! We tried cantering without stirrups, too, which really got me sitting back and down. I could feel Jewel's western spirit coming out then, and I imagined her loping across the countryside after herds of galloping cows. (Do cows gallop? Oh, well, you know what I mean!)

38

The other ponies are totally amazing, too.
Fisher is really laid back, and Danni rides him
so well. Sparkle was still being nervous today,
though. She was especially flighty when we had
to do around-the-worlds, and she skittered
around as Claudia swung her leg up over her

neck. That sent poor
Claudia sliding to
the ground! But even
with dust all over her
jodhs and woodchips
in her hair, she still looked
amazing—typical!

During the lesson, the older girls all kept saying "caramel" in this funny voice and giggling, and when I asked Danni what it was about, she said, "Nothing, just a joke from last night, I can't say in front of Sally." That's when I really, really wished I was sharing a room with them so I could have been in on it.

Afterward, when we were dismounting in the yard and running up our stirrups, Danni said to me, "Sorry you missed out last night, Jess. Sneak in tonight once Tegan's asleep, and we'll have a midnight snack. Oh, and I'll explain about 'caramel.'" That was so awesome of her, and I'm definitely going to do that—there's no way I'm missing out on anything else!

Oh, gotta go, we're due back on the yard— time for our lesson!

I'm writing this in my room,
after swimming and showers

We had such a great lesson, with *another* big
warm-up. (I'm getting used to these now and
not ending up so tired out.) Then Sally split us
into two rides and had us passing hand to hand,
and crossing through X one after the other, so
we could get used to being aware of what each
other was doing, not just ourselves. She said
we'll need that skill for the trail ride when we
won't have a clear track or letter markings to
guide us.

We tried jumping in the second half of
the lesson, doing three combinations, including
a triple. (Sally *still* won't tell us why we
need the practice!) It took Jewel a couple of
tries to get the hang of that, but I kept
giving her tons of encouragement, and
soon we were flying over!

41

My heart was pounding really fast, and I couldn't stop smiling, and it was honestly the best time I've ever had in my life!

So afterward, I was feeling completely over the moon, and I still was when we untacked our ponies and made sure they had fresh water. But then we all gathered for the grooming lecture, and that's when I came back down to earth with a BUMP! *Honestly*, it was as if Tegan couldn't do anything without me, not even tie up Twinkle or pick out his hooves. I'd hoped she was only clingy yesterday because everything was so new and strange, but today she's been worse than ever.

ARGH!

Later on when we all took our ponies up to the field to turn them out, Jewel stayed by the fence, so I hung back for a while. As I rubbed her neck, I told her how torn I feel between taking care of Tegan and spending time with my own friends. Even though she's a pony, at

the exact second I finished speaking,
she snorted and nuzzled my arm, so
maybe she did understand me in a way.

I only meant to be there for a few minutes,
but I lost track of time talking to Jewel, and the
next thing I knew, Sally was tapping me on the
shoulder. She was annoyed at first that I hadn't
come right back with the group and I had to
say I was sorry a *bunch* of times before she
smiled again. I wanted to explain why I'd hung
back, so I ended up telling her what I'd been
talking to Jewel about.

After a while Jewel trotted off to graze,
and Sally and I sat on the fence watching the
ponies roll around, kick their heels playfully, and
munch the grass. "Maybe you should try to see
it differently," she suggested. "I mean, it's kind
of nice that Tegan looks up to you so much.
My little brother just used to fight with me and
hide worms in my sandwiches!"

I smiled at that, but it didn't actually make me feel any better.

"You're doing great with Jewel," she said then. "You've really tuned into her style. She's a free spirit, and you know how to let her be herself. Then she repays you by giving her best because she's so happy."

"Thanks," I said. "I love her so much—she's the best pony in the world."

Sally smiled at that, and then she jumped down from the fence. "Come on," she said. "You'd better get in for dinner." So I followed her, still grinning about the wonderful things she'd said to me.

Great! At last, Tegan has wandered off to find out what the younger ones are doing (she must have gotten bored of fiddling around with her drawing stuff while I've been writing this). I'll just go and see what Danni, Bailey, and Claudia are up to.

☒ Jessica and Jewel ☒

I'm writing this after lights out—luckily I remembered my flashlight!

Tegan's asleep in her own bed as I'd hoped, but I'm still here—sigh! I was really looking forward to sneaking into the older girls' room tonight, but when it came down to it, I just couldn't. I mean, what if T wakes up and finds I'm gone and she's in this dark room all by herself? I couldn't do that to her. So she's fast asleep and I'm stuck here, writing this. I can hear them giggling and whispering down the hall, which is making me feel even worse.

I had a great time with Danni, Bailey, and Claudia earlier, though. I looked in on Tegan, and she was playing with toy ponies in the younger ones' room. (Lola has the biggest collection I've ever seen!) So I got to hang out with my friends—for a little while, anyway.

45

They were all sitting on Bailey's bed, which
is the bottom bunk, with a towel draped down
over it to make a camp-type thing. There was a
ton of giggling and shushing coming from under
the towel. I soon found out why, because when
I joined in, I realized they were talking about
secret girls' stuff. It was so cool, but after only
about twenty minutes, Tegan's head appeared
around the towel. "Jess,
they're all sitting on their
beds now," she whined,
"and each bed is a
separate yard for the
ponies and I don't have
one so I can't play."

Jess!

"Can't you just set yours up on the floor?"
I asked. I mean, ugh!

Tegan gave me a look like I was being
totally crazy. "No, of course not," she said.
"The *beds* are the yards."

I sighed. "Well, maybe you can share with someone," I suggested.

Somehow Tegan managed to hear this as "Come and share with *us*," which is NOT what I meant at all! She climbed right in, chattering away about the pony toys. Even though the girls were really sweet and pretended to be interested, it wasn't the same 'cos we couldn't talk about private stuff anymore (Tegan's much too young for that). I didn't want the others to get bored and annoyed, and after all, it was my fault she was there, so I made an excuse for us to go back to our room.

I ended up sitting on my bed reading *Pony* magazine silently to myself, and when Tegan tried to snuggle in with me, I wouldn't let her.

"You're *mean*, Jess!" she grumped, and then she went up to her bunk and huffed around a lot, making the whole bed shake.

Ugh! I wish she wasn't in a mood with me, but she can't come in here again 'cos I have to get some sleep tonight. It's the trail ride tomorrow, after all! I can't wait—all that riding, all that time to spend with Jewel, and a night camping out under the stars!

I'm going to put this diary down in a minute and go to sleep so tomorrow comes as quickly as possible!

Wednesday—we're just about to go on the trail ride

And guess what? I'm going to share a tent with the older girls!

After we'd had our talk about road safety and first aid, we got our ponies ready. Jewel seems extra sparky today, as if she knows we're off on an adventure! Then we had a break for juice and muffins, and Sally came and told us who'll be in which tent. When she said us four were together, we gave each other an enormous hug.

I was worried Tegan wouldn't be very happy about it and that she might even beg Jess to let me go in with her, so I didn't catch her eye. But she didn't say anything. Instead, she just looked surprised and a little sad. I'm not worrying about it, though—I know she'll be fine, and besides, this is my chance to have my Pony Camp sleepover exactly as I imagined it to be, with secrets and midnight snacks and everything! We're off in a few minutes—this trail ride is going to be SO amazing! I'm even taking my diary with me. It's been a dull day, and Sally said it might rain, so I'm going to wear my riding jacket and slip it into the pocket, along with some candy for midnight snacks!

Wednesday still—we've now set up camp and I'm resting in our tent and writing this while the others go look around

The trail ride to get here was AMAZING and—

Hang on, I'll go back to this morning and start from where I left off.

We all put on our yellow high-visibility vest thingies, mounted up, and set off! I was so excited I couldn't stop grinning! We walked along the road for a really long time, then signaled left to go up a country road. Jess was at the front of the ride, with Sally at the back. Jason and Tyler (Jess's husband and son) were meeting us later at the camping place in the truck, with all the supplies and tents and stuff. As we went on up the road, I got into a comfortable rising trot

on Jewel, and it felt like we were gliding along
with hardly any effort at all. Bailey couldn't say
the same, though! She had to hold Flame back
the whole way with half halts because she was
desperate to go galloping off over the horizon.
Eventually Sally told her to ride tight in behind
Prince. It was so funny because Flame's nose
was almost up his bottom, but it worked and
she stopped trying to break out and settled
into a nice trot.

We went on for quite a while after that,
alternating between walk and trot, and the sun
came out, so I ended up tying my riding coat
around my waist. After another hour or so, we
got into these beautiful cool, shady woods, and it

was really funny because we had to keep ducking
to avoid the low-hanging branches.

Then after another hour or so (I can see why
Sally wanted us to build up some stamina now!),
we stopped off in a field on the other side of
the woods for a picnic. It was only water and
squashed cheese and ham rolls from Jess and
Sally's saddlebags, but we were so hungry and tired
out (especially Lola and Alicia) that it tasted like
the best meal we'd ever had! We all ducked into
the woods to go to the bathroom quickly (not
together, obviously!), and then we were off again.

After some more walking, the track turned
uphill next to a field, and Sally said us older ones
could have a canter with her while the younger
ones trotted on with Jess. Sally warned Bailey to
keep Flame in behind Danni and Fisher and said
no one was to pass her and Blue.

We set off in a nice easy rhythm and it was
wonderful, with Jewel's beautiful mane flying

out and me really sitting into her rhythm. I felt like we were old pros and that we could have been rounding up cattle on the prairie!

But after about 30 seconds, I heard Jess shout, "Tegan! No!"

I glanced around and there was my little sister, cantering with our group. "I want to be with you, Jess!" she cried, a big grin on her face.

I grimaced but I had to focus on my riding, especially as the farther we went up the hill, the more speed our ponies were gathering.

Suddenly, Twinkle was galloping past me, and Tegan's grin turned into a look of terror. She was bouncing around in the saddle, hanging on to the reins for dear life. My stomach flipped over thinking she might fall off and get trampled by one of the other ponies. I wanted to help her, but there was nothing I could do. "Whoa!" she screamed, but Twinkle kept on bolting up the hill, overtaking Bailey and Danni, too.

"Back to trot, girls, please," called Sally calmly, as Tegan came up beside her. Claudia brought Sparkle back fairly easily, and we all slowed down behind her. When Twinkle saw everyone else dropping back into trot, he did the same—phew! On Sally's instructions we dropped to walk, then finally halted and waited for the other group to catch up to us.

Sally had *seemed* calm, but that was only because we were in a dangerous situation. Now that Tegan was safe, Sally was furious with her. So was I. We both shouted, "What on earth do you think you were doing?" but T didn't answer. I could tell she was about to cry.

Jess sighed. "Tegan, that was an extremely dangerous thing to do," she said sternly.

Tegan nodded and sniffled, and it seemed like Sally was about to shout at her again, but then Jess said, more gently, "You must never, ever disobey me, Sally, or any instructor again. Do you understand?"

Tegan nodded miserably, and off we went again.

Luckily, Sally and Jess forgot the whole thing really quickly, and pretty soon we found ourselves in a field with these big logs. Sally explained that they'd been put there as part of a cross-country course by the people who owned the farm up the hill. And then she revealed that we'd needed to practice our jumping because we had permission to try them!

There was a small log that Jess took the younger ones over in trot, following on behind her. We gave them each a loud cheer when

they made it over. Then it was time for us to
try the big one. It was the first time I'd done
any jumping out in the open, and my heart
was thumping with excitement as I watched
Fisher, Flame, and then Sparkle go over
(followed by Sally, to give Claudia an extra bit
of confidence). We cheered for each of them,
too, as they cleared the jump.

When it was our turn, I gave Jewel a big pat,
then gathered up my reins and circled her in trot,
only squeezing into canter as we straightened up.
I didn't want us to end up rushing it.

The log looked so big and solid and for a moment, I thought, *Oh, no, what if she bangs her leg on it?* But there wasn't time to worry.

I just looked past it and trusted Jewel to get us over safely. In fact, we soared over, and Jewel obviously loved it as much as I did because she went charging off in a fast canter on the other side, and I was so surprised I lost a stirrup! But luckily (probably thanks to the balance work we did on Tuesday), I remembered to sit back and down. Then I slowed Jewel with half halts and circling and managed to get it back again. When we went into trot and headed back to the ride, everyone was clapping and cheering.

HooRay!

WOW!

Great job, Jess!

"Good work, Jess! That was excellent!" cried
Sally, and I couldn't help feeling really proud
of myself. We had a few more tries each, and
Tegan and the younger ones had a lot of fun
hopping over the smaller logs in trot, too.

After that, it wasn't far to the campsite. We
did most of it in walk because we were getting
tired out (and so were the ponies). As soon as
we dismounted, Tegan was clingier than ever,
probably because she was still upset about
getting scolded by Sally. After we'd brushed
our ponies down, we had to turn them out in
the next field, and she wanted me to go with
her. I said no because it was only about 50
steps away, and Summer was there already. I
just wanted to spend a little more time with
Jewel. But Tegan kept pestering me until finally
I got really annoyed and snapped, "Fine, come
on!" I stomped off up there with Jewel in
tow, and Tegan following miserably behind

with Twinkle. She'd gotten what she wanted, but she didn't look very happy about it.

I didn't say anything to her while we turned out our ponies, but she kept trying to hug me and was kind of hanging off my neck and going, "Please, Jess, cheer up!"

It was so annoying that I couldn't help shouting, "For goodness' sake, can't you leave me alone for once, Tegan!"

LEAVE ME ALONE!

Her eyes filled with tears. "I'm sorry, Jess," she said quietly, then slunk off toward the tents.

Ugh. I felt like I was right to say that at the time, but writing it down has made me feel really guilty. Poor Tegan. I didn't mean to get that upset. I'll go and find her right now and give her a big hug and say I'm sorry.

Thursday night—back in my bed at Pony Camp!

I've gone to bed early to catch up with my
diary (there's so much to say!). Tegan's so worn
out she's already asleep, even though the light's
still on. Lola and Alicia have gone to bed, too,
but the others are watching something on
Horse and Country TV in the living room.

Well, I suppose I should say what happened
after I went to find Tegan, although
I feel a little ashamed about writing
it down in here.

First, I looked in her tent, and the other
younger girls were there, but she wasn't. Lola
said they hadn't seen her for a while, but I
didn't worry—I thought she must be by the
truck with the older girls, figuring things out with
Jess for our dinner, or maybe collecting wood
for the fire with Jason and Tyler. But I checked

the truck and she wasn't there, and when Jason and Tyler came back out of the bushes with armfuls of wood, she wasn't with them. I could only think that she must have slipped back up to the pony field to visit Twinkle, so I walked over to take a look. "Come on, T!" I called. "We're going to make the fire now."

But she wasn't there, either.

My heart started pounding then, and I felt a little sick. Where on earth was she?

Then I noticed that Twinkle was gone, too.

I raced back to the truck, feeling like I could hardly breathe. "Tegan's gone!" I said, but no one heard above the chatter and laughing. "Tegan's gone!" I shouted. They all stopped talking then. I started sobbing hysterically, and Sally hugged me and told me to take deep breaths and tell her what had happened.

"Tegan's missing and so is Twinkle," I finally managed to stutter. Sally and Jess gave each

other a worried look.
"I upset her, and—"
I began, but then I
broke into sobs again.

"Okay, don't panic,"
said Jason firmly. "I
can take the truck
back down the road to look for her and—"

"But we'd have seen her go by that
way," said Sally. "She must have taken the
bridle path next to the field. And if she's on
horseback, the best way to find her will be on
horseback, too."

"You're right," said Jason. "I'll go."

But Sally insisted that she would. "And I'll
call as soon as I find her," she added.

The way she said that, as if she would
definitely find her, made me feel a little better.
Thank goodness an adult was in control. But
I knew I had to go with her—I just had to. I

was about to try explaining that when she saw the look on my face and instantly understood. "Come on, Jess," she said as she set off for the pony field. Bailey, Claudia, Danni, and Jason came, too, to help catch and tack up Jewel and Blue. "There's one saddle without a bridle here," said Sally, frowning. "Tegan must have gone bareback."

I started crying again then. It would be even harder for her to balance without a saddle and stirrups. What if Twinkle got spooked by something and bolted? What if Tegan got thrown off? I hadn't even checked whether she'd taken her hat or not. She could already be lying in a ditch somewhere, maybe unconscious. I burst into hysterical sobs, wailing, "This is my fault! It's all my fault!"

Sally got very strict with me then. She took me by the shoulders and held me tight. "Jess, if

you want to come, you have to calm down," she
said firmly. "Getting hysterical won't help Tegan.
You need to be positive and focus on finding
her. You can make it up to her then, okay?"

I nodded and sniffled, and even though my
legs were still shaking, I managed to mount up.
Jewel definitely knew something was wrong. She
sprang from hoof to hoof, alert and ready, as if
she couldn't wait to get going. Sally and I set off
in trot and headed down the bridle path. New
worries filled my head as we rode on, things like
what if it got dark and we still hadn't found her?
What would we do then? I pushed them away
and tried to think positive thoughts, as Sally had
told me to, but it was difficult. I tried to look for
clues, but I couldn't see any—there were a lot
of different hoof prints in the mud, but it was
impossible to tell which were Twinkle's. Also,
it was starting to rain again, and the sky had
grown dark with storm clouds.

After what felt like forever, we reached a crossroads with a narrower path. Sally was sure that Tegan would have continued on the main bridle path. I thought so, too, but Jewel was pulling left, wanting to go down the narrower path. I tried to steer her back, but she refused to budge. That surprised me—she didn't usually ignore my requests. "Come on, let's get moving," said Sally.

"I think we should go this way," I told her. "Jewel obviously wants to. I really think she's trying to tell me something."

Sally was about to insist, but something in

my face must have changed her mind. "Okay, we'll go with Jewel," she said.

I leaned down and patted my pony. "Good girl," I told her. "Please lead us to Tegan! Please." I didn't quite believe she'd be able to, but we had to try.

"PLEaSE LEaD us to TEGaN!"

Every time we got around a bend, I kept thinking we'd see Tegan up ahead, but there was nothing, just more thick hedges and slushy mud. If we'd met anyone along the way, we could have asked if they'd seen a young girl riding bareback on her own, but no one came past.

After a while, my confidence in Jewel started to ebb away. Sally's must have, too, because she said, "Maybe we should go back to the main path. If we're on the wrong track, Tegan could be really far ahead by now."

The worry in her voice sent a shudder of fear through me—she didn't sound quite so in control anymore.

We came to another split on the path, and Sally said we definitely needed to turn back then, but my mind was made up. I knew I had to follow Jewel's lead.

"Please, could I just have a minute?" I begged. I tried to calm down, sit still, relax my hands, and *listen.* Jewel whinnied and shifted her weight beneath me. Then I squeezed her on gently, leaving my hands loose and open, letting her choose which path to take. She took the left, and we set off again.

Sally followed after me, but she was already pulling out her cell phone. "We need help," she said, coming to a halt. "I'll call Jess and get her to send Jason and Tyler out along the main bridleway. I'll ask her to call the police, too. And of course, your parents will have to be told."

I felt sick thinking about how
worried Mom and Dad would be,
and how it was all my fault. I slumped
over in the saddle, tears running down my face.
It started raining harder then, pouring down. All
of my positive thoughts completely vanished,
and I felt like there was no hope. "You tried
your best," I told Jewel, "but I shouldn't have
expected you to know which way Tegan went."
But even though my reins were slack, Jewel
continued along the path she'd chosen.

That's when we heard a dog barking up
ahead.

I sat up, listening hard. Sally did, too. Without
a word, we gathered up our reins and trotted
on. When we got over the hill, we saw a
farmhouse.

"I think it's coming from over there," said
Sally. "Dogs usually start up when a stranger
comes near their property. It could be nothing,

of course, but it might be that Tegan is over that way. Come on!"

My heart was pounding, and in my mind I chanted, "Please let it be Tegan," over and over again. Sally had been right when she'd said how lucky I was to have a little sister who liked me and looked up to me. I really was. And all I'd done was push her away. I promised myself that from now on I'd be more patient with her, and include her, and play her favorite board games for hours if she wanted. Anything. Just as long as we found her.

We left the path at the next gap in the hedge and cantered up the edge of the field. The muddy grass was slippery and so were my reins, but Jewel picked out a safe path for us. Then we went right through the middle of a meadow, even though the sign said *Private Property*. As we neared the farmhouse, the dog was louder than ever. But there was a

PRIVATE
PROPERTY

high hedge in front of us, blocking the way. To get around it, we'd have to go all the way back to the path and find another way up.

Sally looked at me. "Do you think you can jump it, Jess?" she asked. "If you follow me over?"

I stared at the hedge. It was huge. I really wasn't sure, but I knew I had to try. It could be the fastest way to Tegan. "Yes," I said.

Sally gave a quick nod, then rode Blue up to the hedge and peered over to check for any hidden dangers on the other side. Then she circled back around in trot. "Okay, follow me."

We trotted on and picked up canter when Blue did, gathering speed. I felt really scared, but I took a deep breath and put my trust in Jewel. Blue did a huge leap over, and as Jewel took off behind him, I held my breath and bobbed forward. And then we'd done it—we were over!

"Great job!" cried Sally as we cantered through the next field.

Up ahead was the farmhouse and the dog we'd heard, a big Alsatian-type. It was running back and forth along the fence line, barking. I felt a little nervous, but Jewel didn't startle.

"Come on," said Sally, and we set off in trot up the pathway in front of the house. We turned a corner and there, huddled under an oak tree opposite some garages, were Tegan and Twinkle. They were both soaked through and my sister was leaning forward, hugging her pony's neck, her shoulders shaking with sobs.

At least she was wearing her hat, though.

"Tegan!" I called.

She jerked her head up and spotted us, then grinned with surprise and relief. But as we got closer, I saw how scared she was. The dog was throwing itself against the fence by then, barking like mad.

WOOF!
WOOF!

As we reached them, I leaped off and handed Jewel's reins to Sally. Tegan slid off Twinkle, too, and we had the longest hug—I didn't want to let her go, ever.

I waited for Sally to scold her—after all, I bet it's the worst thing anyone's done at Pony Camp, ever. That's when I suddenly realized that Tegan might even be sent home early as punishment. Her cold, wet hand slipped into mine, and I squeezed it tight. She knew it, too. But whatever trouble there was, we'd be in it together—the whole thing was at least half my fault, after all.

We were so surprised when Sally just dismounted and hugged us both and asked if Tegan was okay a ton of times.

Tegan nodded. "Bareback riding is harder than I thought," she said. "I kept almost bobbing off in trot, so I had to stick to walk."

"And thank goodness you did!" Sally exclaimed. "Who knows how far you might have gone otherwise!"

"I got stuck because I was scared of the dog," said Tegan, still sniffling. "There's a part up ahead where I thought it could get out under the fence. So we turned back, but I couldn't remember which fork to take on the path, so I had to come back here again. I thought we could wait under the tree until it stopped raining or even wait for the people who live here to come home and help us. I thought we'd be stuck for hours, and I was so scared and lonely. I can't believe you found me!"

"Jewel found you," I told her. "She led us along the right paths. And thank goodness we heard the dog barking—that got us here even quicker. But why on earth did you ride off in the first place?"

"I knew you didn't want me hanging around you, Jess," she mumbled, "and I was really missing Mom and Dad, so I decided to ride home."

"But we live miles away from here!" I cried, shocked.

"I didn't realize," Tegan sniffled. "I thought I knew the way, but then it wasn't the path I'd imagined, and I didn't know what to do." She started to cry again.

I hugged her tight and Sally said, "Well, you're okay, that's all that matters. And I know you'll never do something like this again, not

after the scare you've had. So let's get back to
the camp before we get even more soaked."

"I don't think we *could* get any more
soaked," I said, and Sally and Tegan laughed.

Once Sally had called Jess, we mounted up
and headed back, staying in walk so that Tegan
could balance. When we got to the camp,
we sat in the truck and dried off,
and Jess made hot drinks
for Tegan, Sally, and me
over the gas burner.
As she sipped her
drink, Tegan kept
saying she was sorry
to Sally for going off
when she knew it was completely
against the rules, and to Jess and everyone else
for all the worry she'd caused. Luckily, it was
so obvious how much she meant it that no
one was upset.

It had stopped raining by then, and everyone
crowded around the back of the truck and
made a big deal of us. We told them what had
happened, and I said that Jewel
was a heroine because she'd
led us to Tegan. So the
older girls all insisted on
going up to the pony field
and making a big deal of her, too.

JEWEL
the
Heroine

Soon after that, Jason and Tyler made a
fire, and we cooked hot dogs and
beans over it. They'd brought the
baseball stuff with them, too, and
although we all groaned when
they suggested playing, as soon as we got
started, we found tons of extra energy.

I didn't know whether Tegan would feel up
to playing after her little adventure, but she
was raring to go again. And it was so funny
because whenever Tyler got a home run,

he did this weird victory
dance. We got so giggly
about it that my arms and
legs felt weak, and I could
hardly hold the bat or run!

Tyler

Jess's team won in the end. I was on Sally's,
but I didn't mind!

As it started to get dark, we all gathered
around the fire and toasted marshmallows.
Jason got his guitar out of the truck and we
sang a few campfire songs, squealing as bats
flew low past our heads in the dusk.

As the stars began to twinkle above us,
Bailey and I sang the Sheana song with the
harmonies and everything, and everyone
clapped for us.

Then as it got really dark, we somehow
started telling ghost stories. Danni could be
an actress—she was so good at it! She told
this really SPOOKY one about a car breaking
down late at night in the middle of these
deep, dark woods. She went, "And the girl
suddenly hears a noise on the roof of the car,
like BANG! BANG! BANG!" That made the
younger ones shriek, and Tegan gripped my
arm tight.

Sally then went, "Okay, everyone, I think it's
time for bed!"

Even though I groaned along with the older
girls, I was secretly very relieved!

Tegan wanted to sleep with us, and
of course I said she could after what had
happened. I hardly even *thought* about how
I was missing out on a girly sleepover with
just the older girls, because it didn't seem
important anymore. So we all snuggled in and

chatted about things that Tegan could join in
with, and after about an hour, Sally came in
and said no more talking and good night. We
were waiting until she'd gone to sleep to start
whispering again, but then we actually all fell
asleep ourselves. ZZZZZZZZzzzzzzzzzzzz!

The next thing I remember was Tegan
shaking me awake. "What is it? What's wrong?"
I whispered, all confused because it was pitch
dark and I had no idea where I was at first.

"I need to go to the bathroom," she said.

I sighed and rolled over, trying to go back
to sleep, but she kept shaking my shoulder
until I had to sit up. I didn't want to leave my
nice warm sleeping bag and wander out into
the dark (especially with Danni's scary story
still on my mind!). But Tegan was desperate,
and she refused to go on her own, so I pulled
on my hoodie, climbed over Bailey, and
crawled out.

Tegan wouldn't go on the grass right by the tent. So even though it was spooky, I had to take her into the bushes a bit. I stood nearby and sang quietly to let her know I was still there. "I'm not listening, I'm not listening, I'm not listening," I sang, to a silly tune I'd made up. That made us both giggle. Also, our eyes were getting used to the moonlight by then, so being out in the dark seemed a lot less scary after that.

Back in the tent, we snuggled down next to each other and whispered together in the darkness. After a while of talking about how amazing Jewel and Twinkle are, I asked Tegan why she wanted to be with me all the time.

"I don't want to be with you all the time," she said, "but, well, what if I did suddenly need you and you weren't there? It's best if I stick with you."

That really surprised me—so she didn't enjoy being clingy, either! That's when I realized—she wasn't doing it to be annoying, she just didn't quite have the confidence to go off and do her own thing. And I saw that the way to give her confidence wasn't to push her away—in fact, it was exactly the opposite.

"I bet you'd have more fun hanging out with Lola, Alicia, and Summer in the yard, brushing down your ponies together after your lesson and chatting about the things you did," I whispered.

"Yeah, I would," said Tegan, "then I could borrow Alicia's cool grooming kit."

Jessica and Jewel

I hugged her, sleeping bag and all, and she cuddled into me. "You know, it's fine to go and do things without me, T," I told her. "And I'll make a deal with you. I promise that I'll be there whenever you need me. Just say it, and I'll stop whatever I'm doing. Or if you want to come and join in with me you can do that, too, anytime, and I won't get annoyed, okay?"

Tegan squeezed me tight. "Really?" she whispered. "Thanks, Jess."

We fell asleep soon after that and even if Tegan did wriggle around in the night, I didn't notice. In fact, I was so tired it would have taken a herd of stampeding elephants to keep me awake!

Oh, hang on, I'm just going down to get my hot chocolate—don't want to miss that!

Okay, I'm back! *✶ ✫ ✩*

When we woke up, Sally went to check on the ponies, so we had some time to hang out in the tent. And guess what? Tegan went back into the other tent to play French camping with Lola, Summer, and Alicia. (I don't get how that was any different from the American camping they were actually *doing*, but whatever!) It was so cool because Alicia had poked her head into our tent and asked Tegan to go and play with them. T looked at me uncertainly for a moment, but then she seemed to remember what we'd talked about last night and crawled out, saying, "I'll call you if I need you, Jess."

"Okay. I'll be here," I replied, and I couldn't help grinning.

After a quick breakfast, we took the tents down and packed them in the truck, along with our sleeping bags, night stuff, and fleeces.

Then we collected our ponies, led
them onto the little driveway part, and
gave them a good brush down. As I
tacked Jewel up, I said a big thank you to
her for finding Tegan and told her how good
things were between us now. It didn't matter
if she didn't understand my exact words—she
could see for herself that I was happier and
more chilled out.

We waved good-bye to Jason and Tyler, then
prepared to set off ourselves. As we gave each
other leg-ups and adjusted our stirrups, there

was a lot of moaning and groaning because we were super-stiff from all that riding yesterday.

We took a different route home and us Group B girls had a few awesome canters, which completely took my breath away. And yes, Tegan did behave herself and stay in trot with Jess this time!

Then Sally surprised us all by telling the younger girls that they could do the final canter with us. Tegan looked nervous and excited all at once, but it went fine because she kept Twinkle tucked in behind Prince, as she'd been told to. At the top of the hill, we clapped and cheered really loudly for the younger girls. Tegan looked so proud of herself, and I felt really proud of her, too.

Just when we were almost home, the sky suddenly got very dark, and it absolutely bucketed down with rain. We were all soaked to the skin and squealing and laughing. When we got back to the yard, we put the ponies in the barn, untacked them, and checked that they had enough fresh water. Then we headed straight into the farmhouse to dry off and get changed, and we had a (very!) late lunch of yummy hot tomato soup and grilled cheese sandwiches.

After that, we gave our ponies a really good groom down in the barn, and when the rain let up, we turned them out into the field.

I gave Jewel an extra big pat and hug, and I really didn't want to leave her and go back to the house. She's so beautiful; I'll miss her so much when Pony Camp is over.

Oh, that's the others coming up to bed now. Wow—I can't believe how much I've written!

Friday morning—well, guess what? I got my girly sleepover after all

Once everyone was in bed and the lights were out, I was lying there listening to all the whispering and fun down the hallway. I'd thought Tegan was asleep, but then she told me to go and join in. I said I didn't want to, but she said, "I know you *do*, Jess, and I promise you I'll be fine here. I know I can come and get you if I feel lonely or scared." And so I went! I sneaked back a couple of times to check on her, but she was soon fast asleep.

It was awesome all squashing into the secret camp on Claudia's bunk bed. Me, Bailey, Claudia, and Danni had so much fun!

We told secrets, which I won't write down in here, of course, but I can say I was amazed by what Claudia told us about her BFF! I also found out which one of Danni's brother's friends she has a crush on.

We had a midnight snack of candy that Danni had somehow managed to save until the last night, and talked about private girl stuff, which I'm not going to write down here, either! It was fantastic, and I didn't get back into my own bed until past one o'clock. So I should probably feel tired this morning, but I'm so eager to make the most of my last day with Jewel that I don't at all!

At home again! This week has gone by in a blur!

We've had THE most amazing day!

This morning we had a lesson first thing, only there wasn't a lecture afterward because instead, we needed to prepare for the display we were putting on. It wasn't a real gymkhana or anything, just a fun thing for the parents to watch, showing them everything we've learned this week.

After a break for juice and muffins (which we really needed after that lesson—it's been a scorching day!), it was time to get our ponies ready. We brought them down to the yard and tied them up along the wall. That way Sally and Lydia could help us, and we could all share the kit for making our ponies look extra cool.

Everyone was getting really creative, with
braids in the mane and ribbons in the tail and
even stencils on their ponies'
hindquarters. Sparkle did look
fantastic with the star stencils
on, and Sugar
was cute in glitter
hoof varnish, but I knew
that none of that stuff would
suit Jewel. She's a wild western

glittering Hooves

star stencils

girl, and I wanted her to look that way!

So I did a kind of natural beauty makeover
on her, like they have in girls' magazines, but
a pony version! I gave her coat a really good
brushing until it gleamed, and I used a tiny bit
of this special conditioning spray of Claudia's
to really bring out her rich chestnut color—
she looked amazing after that, like a new
chestnut that had just fallen off the tree. I gave
her legs a good shampoo and carefully wiped

her face marking with the sponge so her white parts really stood out. Then I combed out her mane until it was silky and flowing.

Super Shiny

Combed Mane

All that time, I was telling her how wonderful she was, and how lucky I'd been to have her for my pony, and how much I'd miss her. I had to keep stopping what I was doing to give her hugs!

Then I gave my tack a really good cleaning and wound some blue and white ribbons around her brow band, which looked really pretty. Tegan was on the other side of Lola, and I was just getting Jewel's bridle on when I heard her say she needed to go to the bathroom. I automatically called, "T, do you want me to come with you?"

But instead of saying yes as usual, she
started giggling and said, "Of course not! I can
go by myself. I'm not a baby,
Jess!" The other younger
girls all giggled, too, as if I
was being silly!

I'm NOT a BaBY!

I raised my eyebrows
and said, "Fine, Miss Grown Up, I'm only
asking!" in a pretend moody way, but secretly
I was really happy.

When our ponies were all ready, we put
them in the barn and went to have some
lunch. As we were finishing up our fruit salad,
some of the parents started arriving and
poking their heads around the door. Mom
and Dad didn't appear, so Tegan and me (and
Bailey) helped Jess with the cleaning up.

They still hadn't arrived when the display
was about to start, so Sally let us have a few
more minutes in the yard to wait for them,

and we grabbed our cameras and got her to take some pix of us all together, and standing with our ponies, and then we swapped addresses so we could write to each other (so I now have pen pals—how cool!).

PhoTOS

As we were riding into the manège, Mom and Dad came dashing up from the parking lot. They'd been stuck in traffic and made it just in time!

First, we did a demonstration for about twenty minutes, which was similar to a normal lesson, with Sally calling things out so we could show all the skills we'd learned for the trail ride. The parents were really impressed with

our balance work. And when Sally split the
group in half and got us doing figure eights
riding in between each other, they couldn't
believe there were no crashes. They clapped
really loud at the end and Jewel whinnied with
delight, making everyone laugh.

Then we played a few mounted games,
which were really fun, and the parents all
cheered us on. Jewel and I won the
egg and spoon because she's so
smooth to ride—everyone else's
eggs were going flying, but I hardly
had to even try to balance ours!

For the relay race, Sally said we'd need
to go in twos, an older girl with a younger girl.
I looked right at Tegan, assuming she'd want
to go with me. But she was already waving at
Danni, so I paired up with Lola instead. I was
really happy that Tegan wasn't clinging to me
anymore, but in a funny way, I was a little sad

she wasn't—huh! I never in a million years expected to feel like that!

Me and Lola were up against Danni and Tegan in our heat of the relay race, but we didn't go easy on them because Tegan's my little sister—it was all-out war, and we were determined to win! We actually did, too, but then we lost the second round against Claudia and Summer—oh, well!

After the games, we ran up our stirrups and led our ponies back to the yard to get them some water and untack. Jess brought out some bottles of water and made us all drink, too.

Tegan dragged Mom and Dad around everywhere, and introduced them to Twinkle. It was funny when Tegan showed Dad how to pick out Twinkle's hooves. He's usually

really confident about things, but he looked so
nervous that we couldn't help laughing! And it
was so sweet, because all the time that Tegan

was brushing Twinkle
down, she kept chattering
on about how great I was
at jumping, and what a
good time we'd had on
the trail ride and camp out
(including the going to the

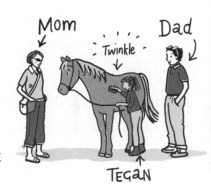

bathroom in the middle of the night part, which
she seemed to have decided was not scary at all
but tons of fun).

Mom came with me into the farmhouse to
get our suitcases, and on the way back to the
parking lot, she said, "Thanks so much for taking
care of Tegan this week, Jess. Oh, and Sally told
us about her little adventure." She raised her
eyebrows and I couldn't help blushing, but she
wasn't upset with me, thank goodness.

"I think you both learned from it,"  she added. "So we'll leave it at that."

Then Mom did something really surprising, which was to say that she and Dad were so impressed with my riding today that they're going to find a way to get me to the more advanced group at my local riding school! "But what about Tegan? You can't go twice," I said.

"We'll work something out," said Mom. "I'm sure we can arrange a carpool. I'll put a card up on the bulletin board at the stables, and until we get something organized, well, I suppose I will have to drive there twice. We can't have you missing out after all your hard work and progress." Well, wow, how about that?! And she hadn't even finished! "Anyway, you deserve a reward for taking care of Tegan so well this week," she said. "We were worried she'd be homesick or too young to manage here, but thanks to you, she had a great time."

"Thanks, Mom," I said. I was really happy about that, although I know I wasn't great to start off with. Still, hopefully I made up for it in the end.

Just then Tegan came running over to us and insisted on pulling her own suitcase along, even though it was on gravel and a little too heavy for her. As she huffed and puffed and struggled with it, she gave me a big grin, and I couldn't help giving her an even bigger one back. Okay, so maybe my week at Pony Camp hadn't turned out exactly as I'd imagined, but looking at my little sister smiling up at me, I realized that I wouldn't have changed it for the world!

Jess x

PONY CAMP
diaries

Learn all about
the world of ponies!

Glossary

Bending—directing the horse to ride correctly around a curve

Bit—the piece of metal that goes inside the horse's mouth. Part of the bridle.

Chase Me Charlie—a show jumping game where the jumps get higher and higher

Currycomb—a comb with rows of metal teeth used to clean (to curry) a pony's coat

Dandy brush—a brush with hard bristles that removes the dirt, hair, and any other debris stirred up by the currycomb

Frog—the triangular soft part on the underside of the horse's hoof. It's very important to clean around it with a hoof pick.

Girth—the band attached to the saddle and buckled around the horse's barrel to keep the saddle in place

Grooming—the daily cleaning and caring for the pony to keep them healthy and make them beautiful for competitions. A full grooming includes brushing your pony's coat, mane, and tail and picking out the hooves.

Gymkhana—a fun event full of races and other competitions

Hands—a way to measure the height of a horse

Glossary

Mane—the long hair on the back of a horse's neck. Perfect for braiding!

Manège—an enclosed training area for horses and their riders

Numnah—a piece of material that lies under the saddle and stops it from rubbing against the horse's back

Paces—a pony has four main paces, each made up of an evenly repeated sequence of steps. From slowest to quickest, these are the walk, trot, canter, and gallop.

Plodder—a slow, reliable horse

Pommel—the raised part at the front of the saddle

Pony—a horse under 14.2 hands in height

Rosette—a rose-shaped decoration with ribbons awarded as a prize! Usually, a certain color matches where you are placed during the competition.

Stirrups—foot supports attached to the sides of a horse's saddle

Tack—the main pieces of the pony's equipment, including the saddle and bridle. Tacking up a horse means getting them ready for riding.

Pony Colors

*Ponies come in many different **colors**. These are some of the most common!*

Bay—Bay ponies have rich brown bodies and black manes, tails, and legs.

Black—A true black pony will have no brown hairs, and the black can be so pure that it looks a bit blue!

Chestnut—Chestnut ponies have reddish-brown coats that vary from light to dark red with no black points.

Dun—A dun pony has a sandy-colored body, with a black mane, tail, and legs.

Gray—Gray ponies come in a range of color varieties, including dapple gray, steel gray, and rose gray. They all have black skin with white, gray, or black hair on top.

Palomino—Palominos have a sandy-colored body with a white or cream mane and tail. Their coats can range from pale yellow to bright gold!

Piebald—Piebald ponies have black-and-white patches—like a Fresian cow!

Skewbald—Skewbald ponies have patches of white and brown.

৩ Pony Markings ৩

*As well as the main body color, many ponies also have white **markings** on their faces and legs!*

On the legs:

Socks—run up above the fetlock but lower than the knee. The fetlock is the joint several inches above the hoof.

Stockings—extend to at least the bottom of the horse's knee, sometimes higher

On the face:

Blaze—a wide, straight stripe down the face from in between the eyes to the muzzle

Snip—a white marking on the pony's muzzle, between the nostrils

Star—a white marking between the eyes

Stripe—the same as a blaze but narrower

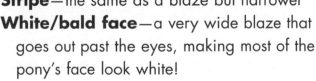

White/bald face—a very wide blaze that goes out past the eyes, making most of the pony's face look white!

Fan-tack-stic Cleaning Tips!

*Get your **tack** shining in no time with these top tips!*

- Clean your tack after every use, if you can. Otherwise, make sure you at least rinse the bit under running water and wash off any mud or sweat from your girth after each ride.
- The main things you will need are:
  — bars of saddle soap
  — a soft cloth
  — a sponge
  — a bottle of leather conditioner
- As you clean your bit, check that it has no sharp edges and isn't too worn.
- Use a bridle hook or saddle horse to hold your bridle and saddle as you clean them. If you don't have a saddle horse, you can hang a blanket over a gate to put the saddle on. Avoid hanging your bridle on a single hook or nail because the leather might crack!

- Make sure you look carefully at the bridle before undoing it so that you know how to put it back together!
- Use the conditioner to polish the leather of the bridle and saddle and make them sparkle!
- Check under your numnah before you clean it. If the dirt isn't evenly spread on both sides, you might not be sitting straight as you ride.
- Polish your metalwork occasionally. Cover the leather parts around it with a cloth and only polish the rings—not the mouthpiece, because that would taste horrible!

Saddle Up!

Find out how much you know about riding equipment with this fun quiz!

1. You should keep your saddle in great condition by:

a. Cleaning it regularly with saddle soap

b. Rinsing it down with hot water after every use

c. Only using it on Sundays

2. The girth is:

a. A strap that goes around the pony's neck

b. A strap that secures the saddle to the pony's back

c. A cool belt to jazz up your jodhpurs

3. When jumping, riders often:

a. Shorten their stirrups a little

b. Lengthen their stirrups a little

c. Cross their stirrups over the front of the saddle

4. The following is NOT a type of bit:

a. An eggbutt, double-jointed snaffle bit

b. A Pelham bit with a rubber mullen mouthpiece

c. A Sanderson super-snazzy bit

5. The following is NOT part of a bridle:
a. The stirrup leathers
b. The cheek pieces
c. The brow band

6. Under the pony's saddle, you should place at least one:
a. Turn-out rug
b. Saddle pad
c. Sandwich for when you get hungry on your ride

7. The following is NOT part of a saddle:
a. The skirt
b. The pommel
c. The dress

8. After every ride, you should always remember to:
a. Rinse your bit
b. Clean your whole bridle
c. Brush your hair

Beautiful Braids!

Follow this step-by-step guide to give your pony a perfect tail braid!

1. Start at the very top of the tail and take two thin bunches of hair from either side, braiding them into a strand in the center.

2. Continue to pull in bunches from either side and braid down the center of the tail.

3. Keep braiding like this, making sure you're pulling the hair tightly to keep the braid from unraveling!

4. When you reach the end of the dock—where the bone ends—stop taking in bunches from the side but keep braiding downward until you run out of hair.

5. Fasten with a braid band!

Gymkhana Ready!

Get your pony looking spectacular for the gymkhana with these grooming ideas!

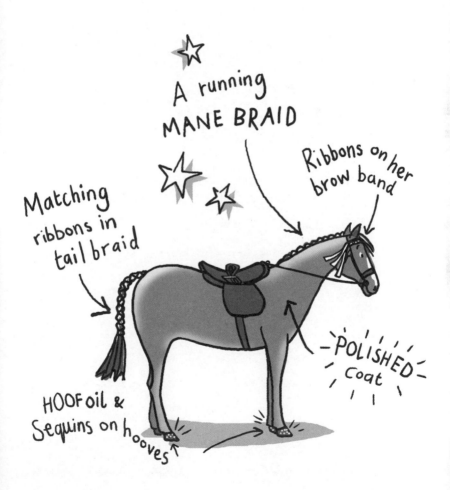

A running
MANE BRAID

Ribbons on her
brow band

Matching
ribbons in
tail braid

POLISHED
Coat

HOOF oil &
Sequins on hooves

Turn the page for a sneak peek
at another story in the series!

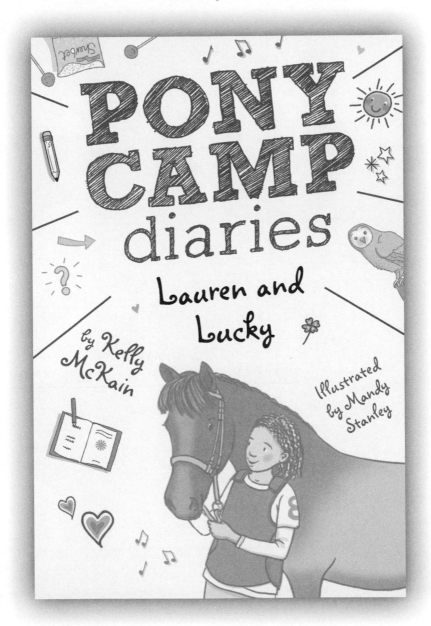

PONY CAMP diaries

Lauren and Lucky

by Kelly McKain

Illustrated by Mandy Stanley

Monday lunchtime—
here I am at Pony Camp!

Us girls are sitting on the benches outside
the farmhouse in the sunshine, and we've all
decided to start our diaries at the same time!
It's been fantastic here so far—I've met all
these awesome girls, been given a fantastic
pony, and we've had our first riding lesson.
Wow! I've just realized that I've got a ton to
say, so I'll try writing really quickly!

By the time Mom and I got here, most
of the other girls had already arrived and
unpacked their stuff. Mom had to rush right off
again 'cos she'd left my three brothers in the
car, so Jess (who runs Pony Camp) showed me
up to my room. All the way up the stairs I was
babbling on about how I'd chosen to come this
week because there's a chance to do dressage.
I've done a few tests at shows near where I live

on Fizz or Gregory, the ponies I ride at my local stables, and I'm really excited about learning more. And it's great 'cos some of the girls here are as dressage-crazy as me! My horsey friends back home are crazy about showjumping instead, so I don't usually get to talk about dressage that much.

When Jess and I got up to the room, the top bunk was already taken by a girl named Arabella, so I took the bottom one. The messy bed by the window turned out to be Jess's daughter Olivia's. She's really nice—in fact, everyone here is.

After we'd said our names, Arabella was like, "Well, the girls in the oldest room all came together, and Olivia will be riding in the other group 'cos she's not into dressage, so *you'll* have to be my friend." I couldn't figure

YOU'LL HAVE TO BE MY FRIEND!

out if she was joking or not, but she just

smiled and put her arm
through mine, and we
went down to the yard
together. That's where
we met the other girls,
and we were all saying
hi and telling each
other what riding
we've done and
that kind of thing.

After Sally showed us around the yard and
gave us a safety talk, it was time to meet our
ponies. We all stood in the yard feeling really
excited as Lydia the stable girl brought them
out one by one and helped us mount up. Sally
said usually we would have an assessment
lesson to figure out which groups we'll be in,
but this week we don't need one 'cos there'll
just be a dressage group and a normal group.

The dressage group (Group B) is:

Paula, age 12, who's Spanish, with **Flame**.

Leona, also 12, whose mom is German and is Paula's best friend, with **Charm**.

Marie, Leona's younger sister, who's 10 like me, with **Mischief**.

Arabella, also 10, with **Gracie**, her own pony (who's a sweet Arab mare with a cute snip on her nose)—how lucky is that!

Me, **Lauren**, and (drum roll, please!) the most gorgeous, cutest pony I have ever seen, my handsome **LUCKY**!

I couldn't believe my luck when Sally said he was for me. My LUCK in getting LUCKY— hee-hee! He's beautiful—a 10-year-old 14hh blue roan cob with a cascading flowing mane, cute clumpy feet, and the most beautiful eyes.

Arabella said, "Lauren, don't you think he's a little too heavy for dressage?" But I just pointed out how well Charlotte Dujardin did on Valegro, who's a heavier build, before he retired. The crowd absolutely LOVED him. Arabella looked a little surprised and muttered, "Fair point."

I gave Lucky an extra pat, just in case he knew she wasn't being very nice about him.

As I said, Olivia is riding with Group A, 'cos she figures her pony, Tally, doesn't exactly get the concept of dressage and is only really happy when he's dragging her through a hedge!

The others in Group A are:

Polly, who is 8, riding **Jewel**.

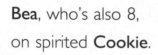

Bea, who's also 8, on spirited **Cookie**.

And **Jojo**, only just 7, on **Sugar**.

 Jess

Sally

Sally taught our group, and Jess taught Group A. We were nervous and excited as we mounted up and made our way to the manège. But we didn't suddenly start doing really hard dressage movements or anything—it was just a normal lesson for Sally to see what we can do.

It was wonderful riding Lucky. He's really chilled out, which is great, but he's not exactly quick off the leg! I'll have to get him to perk up for the dressage test, somehow.

While we were walking around on a long rein to cool down, Sally told us she's got a surprise in store, but she's not going to reveal it until this afternoon. Of course, we were all begging her to tell us right away, but she just did a zipping her lips sign and looked mysterious.

When the lesson finished, we all dismounted and ran up our stirrups, and Sally asked Leona to lead the way back to the barn to untack. Then when we reached the yard, Arabella tried to hand Gracie's reins to Lydia.

Lydia laughed and said, "Nice try, but we all take care of our own ponies here. That's the point!"

Arabella laughed, too, and said, "'Course. Only joking!" But I didn't really know if she was or not. How strange! I'd be desperate to do everything I could for my pony if I had one. Especially if it was my handsome Lucky! I'd do anything for *him*!

Lucky was so funny in the barn. Like when I was grooming him, he kept turning his head and trying to eat the body brush. He also nudged the tack box over with his nose to see if there were any treats at the bottom, probably! I love him so much already, and when I gave him a big pat and rubbed his head, he gave a happy snort and nuzzled into my shoulder, so I think he loves me, too.

Arabella was waiting by the barn door for me so we could go in for lunch together, but

I had to keep popping back to see Lucky! She just stood there, going, "Hurry up, I'm hungry!" so I gave him one last hug, and then I gave Gracie one, too, so she didn't feel left out.

For lunch we had chicken and salad and—

Oh, we're all off to the yard now. Sally's going to reveal her surprise! Well, fast writing worked, 'cos I got down almost everything we've done so far!

If you love animals, check out these series, too!

Pet Rescue Adventures

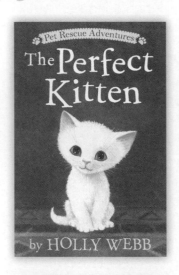

Pet Rescue Adventures
The Perfect Kitten
by HOLLY WEBB

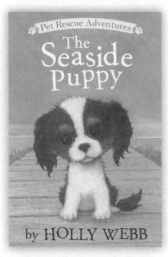

Pet Rescue Adventures
The Seaside Puppy
by HOLLY WEBB

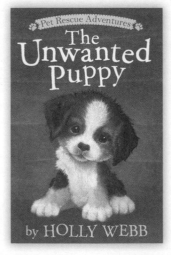

Pet Rescue Adventures
The Unwanted Puppy
by HOLLY WEBB

Pet Rescue Adventures
The Kidnapped Kitten
by HOLLY WEBB

ANIMAL RESCUE CENTER

ANIMAL RESCUE CENTER

The Abandoned Hamster

by TINA NOLAN

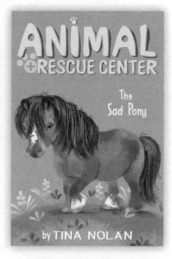

ANIMAL RESCUE CENTER

The Sad Pony

by TINA NOLAN

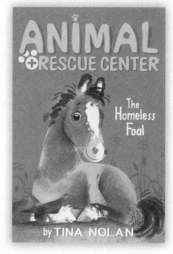

ANIMAL RESCUE CENTER

The Homeless Foal

by TINA NOLAN

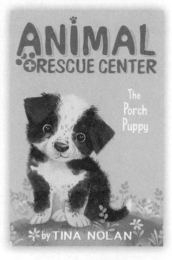

ANIMAL RESCUE CENTER

The Porch Puppy

by TINA NOLAN

Kelly McKain

Kelly McKain is a best-selling children's and YA author with more than 50 books published in more than 20 languages. She lives in the beautiful Surrey Heath area of the UK with her family and loves horses, dancing, yoga, singing, walking, and being in nature. She came up with the idea for the Pony Camp Diaries while she was helping young riders at a summer camp, just like the one at Sunnyside Stables! She enjoys hanging out at the Holistic Horse and Pony Center, where she plays with and rides cute Smartie and practices her natural horsemanship skills with the Quantum Savvy group. Her dream is to do some bareback, bridleless jumping like New Zealand Free Riding ace Alycia Burton, but she has a ways to go yet!